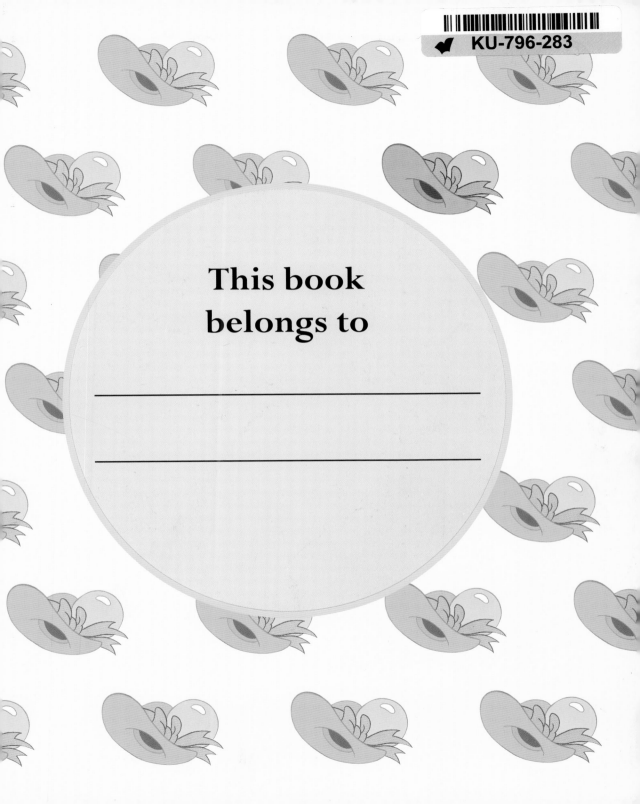

This book belongs to

_____

_____

First published by Parragon in 2012
Parragon
Queen Street House
4 Queen Street
Bath BA1 1HE, UK
www.parragon.com

ISBN 978-1-4454-7085-6

Printed in China

MINNIE MOUSE
A Magical Story

by Ann Braybrooks
Illustrated by Len Smith and Arcadia

Bath · New York · Singapore · Hong Kong · Cologne · Delhi
Melbourne · Amsterdam · Johannesburg · Auckland · Shenzhen

It was a perfect Spring day and Minnie Mouse was spending it in the perfect way – she was making a new bonnet!

"Not bad," Minnie said, admiring her new bonnet.
"But it's not what I had in mind."

Minnie searched her closet, her dresser drawers and her cabinets until she found just the thing...

...an old bag of balloons! Minnie quickly blew up two –
one pink and one yellow. Then she removed the feathers
and tied the balloons to her bonnet with pretty lavender
ribbons.

As Minnie was putting the final touches on her new creation, she spotted Mickey Mouse through her window.

"Yoo-hoo, Mickey!" she cried, running outside. "I want to show you something!"

Suddenly, a gust of wind snatched up the balloons – and Minnie's beautiful new bonnet sailed up into the sky!

Minnie quickly jumped in Mickey's car and fastened her seatbelt.

"Follow that hat!" she cried.

Mickey and Minnie drove through town, keeping their eyes on the floating bonnet. Minnie held her breath every time it drifted near telephone poles and chimneys – but the bonnet just soared higher into the sky with each fresh gust of wind.

"Oh, no!" Minnie cried. She watched nervously as a curious crow flew right towards her bonnet! The bird began pecking at the pink balloon and...

...POP! The startled crow flew off.

There was only one balloon left, but the bonnet was still floating high in the air.

Mickey and Minnie drove to the edge of town, following the bonnet as the wind carried it farther and farther away.

Soon they reached a farm and Mickey spotted a rope hanging from a fence post.

Mickey grabbed the rope and tied it into a lasso.
One... two... three times he tossed the lasso into the air.
But the bonnet was still out of reach.

The hat zigged and zagged over the farm, until the yellow
balloon snagged on a weather vane on top of a barn. POP!
"Oh, dear!" cried Minnie as she watched the bonnet drop…

...right into the branches of a tall tree.

"We've got it now!" Minnie cried. "Help me with this ladder, Mickey!"

While Mickey held the ladder, Minnie carefully climbed up and found…

...a robin redbreast sitting in her hat!
"Hey, that's not a nest!" Minnie said to the bird. "Shoo!"
But the robin was quite comfortable and wouldn't budge.

Suddenly, the robin was joined by another robin!
"Oh, I see," Minnie said, admiring the happy couple. She
tried to be very quiet as she climbed down the ladder.

"I should have suspected that it would end this way," Minnie sighed.

"What do you mean?" Mickey asked.

"After all," Minne said with a laugh, "That bonnet has been nothing but trouble!"

The End